These Hands

Written *by* Hope Lynne Price • Illustrated *by* Bryan Collier

Jump at the Sun

Hyperion Paperbacks for Children
New York

These hands
can touch.
These hands
can feel.
These hands
create.
These hands
can build.

These hands
can reach.
Can stretch.
Can teach.

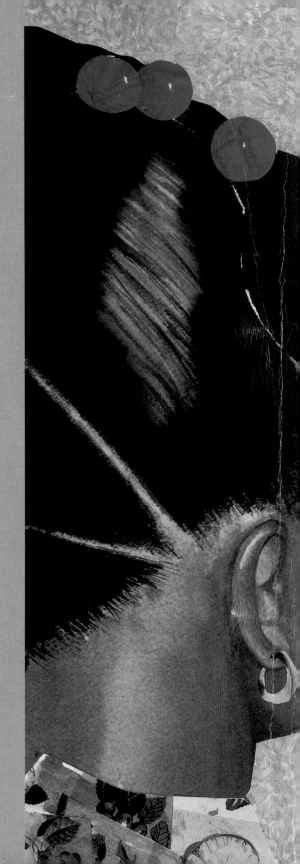

These hands
can hug.
Can pat.
Can tug.

These hands
  can squeeze.
Can tickle.
Can please.

These hands can hide something inside.

These hands
can write.
Can fly a kite.

These hands
can talk.
Help Grandma
walk.

These hands
can read.
Can share.
Can feed.

These hands
can shake
you wide
awake.

These hands
can pray.
Can clap.
Can play.

Can sow the
seeds
for a brighter
day.

To Noli and Jordy, with love from Mom —H.L.P.

To the Meyers family, with love and thanks! —B.C.

Text copyright © 1999 by Hope Lynne Price
Illustrations copyright © 1999 by Bryan Collier

Printed in Hong Kong
First Jump at the Sun paperback edition, 2007
1 3 5 7 9 10 8 6 4 2
This book is set in Gill Sans 48/60.
Library of Congress Cataloging-in-Publication Data on file.
ISBN-13: 978-1-4231-0633-3
ISBN-10: 1-4231-0633-4

Visit www.jumpatthesun.com